Pocketful O' Stories 3.0

T0014998

PENGUIN
ENTERPRISE

An imprint of Penguin Random House

PENGUIN ENTERPRISE

USA | Canada | UK | Ireland | Australia
New Zealand | India | South Africa | China

Penguin Enterprise is part of the Penguin Random House group of companies
whose addresses can be found at global.penguinrandomhouse.com

Published by Penguin Random House India Pvt. Ltd
4th Floor, Capital Tower 1, MG Road,
Gurugram 122 002, Haryana, India

First published in Penguin Enterprise by Penguin Random House India 2022

Copyright ©

ISBN: 9780143457527

Typeset in Myriad Pro
Printed at Thomson Press India Ltd, New Delhi

www.penguin.co.in

Preface

Love happens when you least expect it. All it takes is a smile or a glance to fall madly in love. And Engage is all about love. With its vast range of fragrances that includes Deo Sprays, Perfume Sprays, Premium Perfumes and Pocket Perfumes, Engage creates enchanting moments of romance and playfulness between lovers. What keeps the romance alive and sizzling is the unexpected twist and turn.

Engage celebrates these beautiful and unplanned moments of love that has taken a renewed form of love in present day. Be it old school love or romance in the new normal, Engage's range of fragrances ensures that you smell right and makes every unpredictable moment of romance with your loved one special.

Flip through the pages and be mesmerized by the most magical and spontaneous moments of love.

Lockdown fated, the two busy neighbours bump into each other. From sharing kitchen ingredients to sharing life, they unlocked a new level of life--love. They wondered why they never communicated before. Guess it takes just a moment to ease down from our bustling lives and knock the door, of hearts.

ankitaaaher

Living apart for another year was certain. So, we understood more than we talked, we felt more than we heard. From morning cup of coffee to bedtime kiss, we cherished every moment of love we dreamt together for us . . . before we could meet again to hold the hands and walk amidst the starry nights. Something we always wished as we met and yet another year, 2020, didn't change anything for us. ❤

wimple_kaur

We both waited for our flight with masks on and leaving chairs in between for social distancing. Afraid to talk to people, we both just gazed at each other. We were silent, but the eyes talked a lot with the stranger, beholding the smiles behind the masks. Social distancing couldn't stop their hearts from coming close. Numbers were exchanged and our flight landed with love in midst of a pandemic.

poulamie13

2020 taught us that romance was all about the small efforts we made to hold onto each other, even in the darkest times. From going to the morning walks together to working out on video calls. From spending hours together to calls and messages, love was indeed heartbeats measured in miles.

charulkandoi09

It was not our anniversary, neither my birthday nor his, yet at the hour that struck midnight, a tub of ice cream and and some delicious brownies delivered to my place to deal with my mood swings, all around when human touch and physical contact died, even through distances, we kept our spark alive.

_aishiki_b_

This year our romance was eyes that would see, but hands that could not touch . . . ears that would hear, but lips that could not meet . . . physically, we may have been "socially distanced", but our hearts were locked, beating as one, across the digital screen. ❤

hued_soliloquy

Every love fights its battles. We had to fight a little extra this year. I, with my stethoscope and she, with her police uniform, fought the battle of distance. Then we fought the virus. This year taught us 'how staying apart can also be love'. With new lessons, now there will be new year, new us.

avya_apeksha

You're the kind of boy I wished to write poetries about. Entangle your hair with metaphors of love and rhyme them with trust. Alliterate our smiles with ironies of life. Hence, I wrote one. You, being my lost love texted me saying, "I missed your poetries!" While I replied, "I miss the one my poetries were about." The long-lost love found its home in words again and that's how our romance rekindled.

harshitagupta_16

Timezones apart but we still feel the love. In the midnight calls and the heartfelt messages. In the poems he writes for me and the letters I write to him. My nights are his mornings but we make it work. Because the distance never matters, because the heart wants what it wants. ❤

mahima_shilpa

Prepared for the cheesy pick-up lines and fake similes by random guys, I gave in to online dating to curb my lockdown boredom. Little did I know that one unintentional swipe would change my life forever, leading me to my special someone. The virtual dates with him were as comforting as having an ice cream sundae on a warm summer day or sipping a spiced hot chocolate on a cold winter night.

gugs92

There's excitement to see him, after all these months spent in solitude. To feel his skin against mine, the eagerness to hold his hands again and to see the crinkle in his coffee bean eyes when he smiles. His eyes always smile when he looks at me. In my heart, I know there's a chance I'll fall in love with him all over again.

jayne_nidhi

First time on a virtual date with him, I dressed up and waited for him on the screen. After 5 minutes he appeared and smiled at me. He was wearing the black shirt that he wore on our first (in person) date. It reminded me of our first kiss and that still gives me butterflies!

dishasahijani

Timezones apart but we still fix everything. Still your alarm ring wakes me up here and my bed stories makes you warm there. I still pray for us with rising sun and you still wish for us with shooting stars. Your virtual kiss still makes me warm, your video calls still hold me up and your love still marks your presence here. My Love, near or apart, you'll be always in my heart!

lakshita_writes

Our favourite part about the lockdown opening up was the long drives we had. During the lockdown, with each video call and text, we realized the value of spending time together. Some may say that closeness is what we lacked but our love was still steamy at the end of every video call; we made sure to say, "I love you."

mayankrajai

What makes our romance special is that it isn't just filled with hugs, kisses and butterflies. Our love is like the old T-shirt which fits you perfectly. Sure it is not perfect with coffee stains on it, but you can't even think of replacing it. It is comfortable and cozy. Isn't that what love is really about? Being comfortable to show your ugliest demons and share the craziest stories with?

aishwarya_jayakrishnan

She was an introvert. Only texted back with emojis. But when she started talking to him, she started feeling different. His replies never failed to give her goosebumps and a shy smile. He could understand her feelings and emotions behind each of those emojis. That's when replies came in paragraphs, but only to him.

_.daydreamin.___

From sharing memes to finally setting up a virtual date for the first time. It was a candle light dinner over a video call. We talked so much that I never noticed how time passed by so quickly and I fell asleep. I got up the next morning to her adorable sleeping baby face on the screen and we ended our dinner date with breakfast.

tnt31097

From sharing memes to finally making her mine, I couldn't be more grateful to technology. For a shy introvert like me, it was through the memes that I conveyed my messages to her. Her being a good decipherer, she understood my love

gkgokul18

ENGAGE

It was all merry when a box with a fuzzy blanket, a Charles Dickens book, a packet of hot chocolate and a note was dropped off in from my door. The note read, "Join me for a virtual christmas date, all the essentials are included in this box. 2020 cannot make us celebrate Christmas apart." @durjoydatta @engagebyitc #romanceunlocked #engagepocketstories #RomanceUnlocked#EngagePocketStories

nidhijohari_

"How do I look?" I asked him. "Pretty as ever", he smiled and replied. "Shall we?" he requested while extending his hand towards me. "Yes, please", I giggled. With our favourite song playing in the background, we danced. He in his room and me in mine, watching each other through a video call. And that's how our romance rekindled. @engagebyitc #EngagePocketStories #RomanceUnlocked

divya.garg.54

Meet request sent,
Virtual date, first for her.
She lost her breath, butterflies in gut, when her face
appeared on the screen.
A single mother got a chance to fall in love all over
again.#RomanceUnlocked #EngagePocketStories
@engagebyitc

priyan_she_

Two cups of coffee on a chilly morning or a drive to
our favourite food joint to eat that hot plate of momos
is what romance for me is like, because I'm not that
much of a person who shows love, but this lockdown
taught me that a long phone call in the night on our
terrace while gazing at the stars and full moon can
be much more beautiful. 💜 #engagepocketstories
#romanceunlocked

neelubathla

ENGAGE

On a Christmas night, she meets a soul loveless, but she sees he's waiting to shower all the love on one that deserves. He didn't care who's around and was happy on his own and swept her off her feet unknown. She's told to step back as he's not the one, but she's sure if anyone's worth all the fight, it's him and none. A year of LDR waiting to see each other in real, 2 souls could never stay apart, so surreal.

mounika_210

"Let's have a picture together", she said. Then he said, "How's it possible? We are 1000 km far from each other and I'm badly missing you." She said, "Just imagine I'm with you and we'll take a perfect screenshot selfie."
Both smiled.
Screenshot taken.
Beauty of long distance relationships. And that's how they survived the lockdown beautifully.

yukta_pareek

Inside the house you're doing your time,
Being faraway from me is your only crime.
You're my star, you're my moon, being with you will
come very soon.
My love, in your absence, I buried my nose in your shirt.
Which takes me to the times we spent together.
Though we are far in miles,
But I have your shirt to make me smile.

nainashah_26

2020 taught me that he too deserves surprises and
pampering even if they're in the form of a crooked
tasteless cake, handmade origami anniversary cards or
just a peck on his cheek before we say, "Good night!"

storiesbysurabhi

I resolved to take an off from my chamber routine on Tuesday for my chronic allergy that effed me up really bad on Diwali. I woke up at 4 pm and he stunned me with his wish to drop by. I longed to see him, but I was sick enough to go out. He had to hang around for over 120 mins to get a glimpse of me waving from my balcony. That Shakespeare balcony scene was recreated and that's how our romance rekindled.

twinklenextdoor

I always hated her for highlighting textbooks until one day before our 'English literature' virtual exams, she sent her book, highlighting only three words. The thing I hate the most about her became a memorable one forever.

contemporary_literary_threads

I decided to start a writing blog and pour down my thoughts. I was never good at expressing my feelings but my pen was. They always asked me, "Did you confess or are you still shy to?" But things happen when they are meant to be and that day, he started following my blog and left a comment, "I wish I had someone who wrote this for me." And I replied, "I wish you knew that your wish has already come true."

harshitagupta_16

It was love at first sight which made them turn head to toe in love with each other. While she thought of it as infatuation, he was determined in trying his luck for the only girl he ever loved. He gave her a helping hand, had her back, made sure of her safety and took all the care. It took time before they became best friends. Friendship worked, so did their brewing love.

dhruv_dc_

ENGAGE

Our love in 2020 was like a tale of seasons. Summers arrived and we were locked inside. Clear and blue like the skies, our love felt new. Autumn leaves felt like me, fell for you even more. Winter played its card, love held us hard. Spring arrived and a little flower bloomed in our heart, we called it ours. 2020, the year full of scars and stars.

harshitagupta_16

16 years and there won't be a day, we won't meet. He would call it 'love' and I, 'habit'.
I always said, "We won't be so attached if we ever have to stay apart."
Then lockdown happened and it's been 103 days, I haven't met my 'habit'.
But the attachment is still there, even stronger now.
I guess he was right about the feeling.
Staying apart, lockdown or 2020 didn't change anything for us.

rang.hinai

To my serendipity
With our undivided attention in 2019,
and staying apart in lockdown in 2020,
from valentine to quarantine, ✷
Love has never gave up on us.
I still wonder how we successfully shifted,
our real date to a virtual one and enjoyed every moment of it.
Yes, I can proudly sum up,
2020 didn't change anything for us.
P.S. With every passing day, our innocent love grows stronger.

priyankajha

From watching movies together on dates to watching them
on Netflix party . . . 2020 didn't change anything for us. ❤

palak.chawlaa

We still talk a lot, behave like idiots sometimes, meet daily, go on dates, have fun, smile a lot. Your smile is still as beautiful as it was. It's just that even though you are always present with me, I badly miss you and your presence. I still look up at the sky and whisper your name. Don't worry, I have preserved your smile in my heart. Ultimately, 2020 didn't change anything for us.

prama_8

Our love in 2020 is so fresh that it still feels like 2010 when for the first time, you held my hand in our school bus, making sure no one gets to know and now holding my hand as we exchange rings and making sure each person knows, "That I'm yours, forever."

akanksha_sharma07

Those 3 am conversations happened on every Saturday when we didn't fear about getting up early the next morning. It was the only time when our sleepy conscience allowed us to talk our heart out, fight like little kids and cuddle like we never did. This midnight routine got along with it, a euphoria of heartfelt emotions and became a part of our love life.

dhruv_dc_

'Distance makes heart grow fonder,' they say, but distanced in relationships make them grow far away. Living away and living together has its own problems, from surprises to spending time together, you wish to spend sometime alone, from video calls every day to no topics left to talk. Yet in these times, from having dinner together to never watching finale of web series alone, they sail together.

_thoughts_unplugged

The lockdown was our nightmare. Married for years, we were running away. But now we didn't have a choice. To survive, we had to understand each other, and that's when it happened for us the second time. Love.

Durjoy Dutta

She was too pretty, he was far from it.
A perfect 10, and a measly 5.
The virus gave her enough time to discover,
that he was a solid 15.

Durjoy Dutta

Childhood lovers. Stayed far away. She decides to go farther away for studies.
One night before leaving the country, she texts, "Please meet."
5 minutes before boarding. Her eyes scanned for him. He wasn't there.
But a man came running and handed her a parcel with a note: "Surprise! Open after the plane takes off."
35,000 feet above the ground, his gesture made her fall in love, again.

anubhab.pati

2020 taught us that romance can start in the grocery store, at the fruit aisle, while sharing glances! 2020 taught us that quarantine drives and movie marathon the entire night can bring two hearts closer and make them grow fonder! 2020 taught us that love is not enough to keep the relationship alive, you need much more than that!

arorasamridhi

2020 taught us romance has no age. As time passed, me and Arjun had lost those tiny moments we always cherished. Waking up to a kiss, enjoying silence with smile, working in same space, exchanging secret stares but when we both were locked together in the lockdown, these small things made the tough time little better, making us understand even a small smile of our love can comfort us beyond the limits.

writing_photography_keethu

2020 taught us that romance was all the "I love you's" his eyes whispered which his mouth couldn't beneath the mask. It was embracing your loved ones beyond touch, either 6 feet or 6 countries apart. It was attending the virtual class only to meet his eyes once in a while. It was a quick run to the grocery store for the packets of maggi, only to find him shopping for the same.

siddhigangan98

2020 taught us that romance isn't bound by walls, it's like a breeze, it will find a way to flow. The lockdown couldn't stop those two from talking the whole night . . . it couldn't stop them from texting the entire day . . . they missed each other but in the end, it only made their love stronger . . . they discovered that no matter how far they are, the scent of their romance will definitely reach the other one.

bhoomiabichandani_

With hopes bending, lives surrendering, seeing some romances burn to death, and us from a million miles apart still coping with the chapter of love, we kept the spark alive.

_pooja_talwar

The lockdown hit us hard. Every day, I would ache for his touch, his scent, his kisses and his tight hugs.
He would send me brownies to lift my mood and I would get his favourite ice cream delivered. While I would write and recite poems about our love story, he would compose songs for me and sing them during video calls.
The pangs of separation hit every now and then but we kept the spark alive.

srishtification

Chosen as dance partners for every performance at school, even they didn't realize when their hearts started beating to cupid's love song. Not until the time when schools didn't open for months and they knew it wasn't just the dance that they were missing. First love is indeed difficult to understand. But with a virtual date and long phone calls, the two dance partners were now life partners.

the_shortprose

After getting to know each other over texts, they finally decided to meet but lockdown happened.
"A virtual date?" he asked.
Being camera conscious, she hesitated but gave in.
With a racing heart and trembling fingers, she swiped the screen up to take the video call.
"God! You look so cute with these glasses, I'm dead." was the first thing he said and all her fears turned into butterflies.

rang.hinai

"Are you ready for the movie night?" he asked. "Born ready!" she replied. It was 11 pm at night and Netflix made their first virtual date night successful. In this lockdown, people are apart but hearts are not.

avilashawrites

Our first virtual date never felt virtual, but more than real. Though there was no soothing touch of his on my skin, I felt every bit of emotion running through my veins, which I felt more pronounced than before. With my messy hair, dark-circled eyes, he, sipping coffee and gazing at me on Skype, we felt the real meaning of romance.

nikshepa_chunchula

A planned video call night on our terrace, under a million stars, lost in our work, but stealing eye contacts like a lover stealing stars. Best friends not lovers, for we never knew if the other one craved for it too. Lost in the depth of us, I sang, "I wish the universe in you falls in love with all the galaxies in me." And he replied, staring at me, "I am a star that has already fallen for you."

harshitagupta_16

From sharing memes to finally sharing a bedroom, our "2 states" love story has been nothing less than a roller coaster ride for the two of us. However, laughing with him at random memes today often makes me wonder. Maybe our story wouldn't have started if these memes didn't act as the perfect conversation starters for two introverts like us.

_shwe_writes_

From sharing memes to finally getting a sudden confession in between a Ludo game, our love started amidst nationwide lockdown. We both feared long distance relationships but by reading old chats, locking our eyes in video calls, turning hugs into gifs and kisses into emojis, we kept our spark alive.

prama_8

From sharing memes to finally making it to their wedding day, two best friends knew that they were meant to be together. "Aren't you nervous?" he asked her, "nervous only about now I have to see your ugly face every morning for the rest of my life," she replied with a wink. "You have one last chance, think about it," he said. "What to think about it? Everything is fair in love and war," she giggled.

jhawarrr

It was all merry when we held the hands walking through the bridge to share a kiss before parting away for the day and turned even merry when we held the hands through the screen sharing a kiss and fall asleep in the middle of important conversations. Waiting for your return so we could bake plum cake and celebrate Christmas because with you it always gets merrier than ever. Merry Christmas, love!

writing_photography_keethu

This year our romance blossomed over messy kitchen, heaps of laundry and Netflix series. From sharing the workload to munching on the popcorns, understanding the essence of togetherness within the closed doors was a highlight of our love life this year.

seemaswastika

We were just learning to swim in the river of love when the entire world was surfaced under lockdown. Afraid of love fading away like the rainbow in the twinkling of an eye, we decided to keep the spark alive. With every passing day, learning and understanding each other, love proved to be just a test of time. For standing strong through the turmoil of emotions, here's to a new beginning.

charulkandoi09

Whatever happens in 2021, I know you will always stand by my side. The roller coaster ride that 2020 was will be a lifelong acquaintance. Sharing our darkest secrets to the fun banters, the petals of our relationship bloomed with each passing day. Still, there's a long way along but now our souls are emotionally engaged. Cheers to now and forever!

mitalisehgal13

Our love resolution is to travel the world together--nature, good food, books, music, repeat. Travelling had always been our passion and how can I ever forget when with the sunrise, our eyes met at 5400 feet, when valley of heaven was under our ground as it was over our heads on the highest peak of Maharashtra, Kalsubai Mountain. Happiness is doubled when shared with you.

dr.shweta_sachdeva

Childhood sweethearts, we became so used to each other's presence in our lives that romance took a backseat.
With lockdown announced and him being on a trip to the Himalayas with minimum network coverage. We waited for hours to connect on a video call or send or receive pictures, so we wrote poems and long romantic paragraphs telling each other how much we love. That's how our romance rekindled.

rang.hinai

We were on the terrace sipping our late night coffees when she exclaimed, "See, it's a full moon today!" I looked at the big white moon above and closed my eyes. "Are you even listening to me?" she complained. "How I wish I could see that pretty face of yours glowing under this perfect moonlight." I whispered into my phone's speaker. Miles away, her heart smiled and that's how our romance rekindled.

the_shortpose

Timezones apart but we still know how to make each other's heart flutter hard. "I feel lonely with you not being here", she sighed and ended the call. I decided to record videos of me reading books to her so that she feels less lonely at nights while she sang for me and sent the videos when I felt depressed. We found our love in recorded videos with sleepy faces, tired voices but happy hearts.

harshitagupta_16

Timezones apart but we still manage to start our days with each other's heavy morning voices. In the world full of digital messages, we still post handwritten letters. And at the end of the day, while you sleep with me on a video call, I am my most peaceful self. Because even though miles apart, you still bring out the best in me.

that_imaginator

Timezones apart but we still read each other's hearts. I know when he is upset over a bad day at work and he knows when I am stressed for my exams. The moment we see each other's face on the screen, a wave of calm washes over us. We will forever be connected, not by touch but by words. No distance can break us because the heart wants what it wants! ❤

mahima_shilpa

The obstacles after getting into labour during the nationwide lockdown was immensely a tough situation for both of us. But he made sure to never take off his hand from my shoulders and I made sure not to lose hope. While he made his way all inside me to bring a life into this world, I was in my happy place to get a doctor as my life partner and a child who made me a mother.

cdeblina17

I was browsing through the comic section of the bookstore. I saw you from the corner of my eye, walking towards me. "Excuse me, can you help me find a comic for my nephew", you said, looking at me shyly. "Of course", I said giggling. 10 years later, as we were having coffee in bed, you told me, "That was actually just an excuse to talk to the girl browsing through the comic section." ❤

menenners

Our story is adventurous and wild, we lose each other multiple times but also find back each other. As if it's like the earth's magnetic force, which tries to bring us back together. I write a thousand words on you but you never even bother to read them, still I write about you and for you with the hope that when we find back each other again, you will read them.

aliva.dutta

Our story is an adventurous tale of two losers stuck together in the Salsa class. I did step on his feet quite a lot, he dropped me more than a few times and we did share some laughs. Though at times we looked silly, he picked me up again and I continued to hold onto him. For the magic to happen at love and dance, one has to let one's heart have some fun, even at the risk of embarrassing oneself.

jayne_nidhi

I saw her at the supermarket, while everyone around was busy shopping, she was standing at a corner struggling with her mask and spectacle. At once she cleaned the fog on the glass and the next time she tried to fix her mask. I fell for the Innocence In her eyes against the battle of struggle. It was love at masked sight.

___.e.s.t.r.e.l.l.a.___

Busy studying always, I never knew how to cook. My mom asked me, "Will you only cook Maggi in the name of food?" and I always laughed hard. 5 years later, when she asked him, "What made you fall in love with her?", he replied, "Maggi." Whenever I felt stressed, she made me Maggi. Although it took her more than 2 minutes to cook but less to make me smile and cover the distance between our hearts.

harshitagupta_16

"What happens when two poets fall in love?" they asked. "They become a poetry for each other!" he said with a wink. "Your smile is my soul food and the colourful hues to my blues!" I smiled and replied, "No matter the distance, I'll always end up beside you, just like the sea waves return back to the shore, I've drowned in the depths of you!" Poetry became our language when love equated with YOU.

harshitagupta_16

Two foodies in love. Their weekend date nights involved wandering in streets holding hands in the hunt for yummiest delicacies. Lockdown stopped their ritual. First Saturday of April, 8 o' clock sharp, their doorbells rang at the same time. She received biryani and he, momos from their favourite food joint. Distance of 9 miles couldn't stop them to have home delivered their favourite food and love.

rang.hinai

Indeed during this lockdown, I was blessed to have tasty homemade food every day but what I still missed and craved for the most is that '*Aate ka Halwa*' which he used to cook with loads of ghee, less sugar and all his love, just the way I like and he would bring that for me every time we used to meet. This distance surely made me miss the smallest things that he did for me.

__shreya_bajpai__

She made dinner for him and he baked a chocolate cake for her. She wore his favourite coloured dress while he wore her gifted hoodie. Up until the dinner time came, they both waited eagerly to surprise each other. Stuck in the same city, far away from each other, distanced by a shared screen, it was the best anniversary they celebrated.

cdeblina17

Being an old school romantic, I have always loved the idea of love. Letters, long drives, dried flowers have always been my favourite. Scared to propose my bestfriend, picking rose petals and FLAMES became my escape. "Meet me at the library!" he texted me. While smiling nervously, he asked, "Will you be my bestfriend and lover for lifetime?" and gifted me a keychain with our initials intertwined.

harshitagupta_16

We had met just once and the only thing common we had was our favourite song. Today our arranged marriage turned 1. So during our long drive, our favourite song came on radio and made us recall our first meet. He said, "One thing has changed." "What?" I questioned, to which he replied, "You are now on top of my favourites' list."

avya_apeksha

What makes our romance special is the fact that neither of us proposed each other. Yet we know that we both are in love. Those sudden surprise moments, those stares and those accidental lovely touches . . . makes our romance special!

pampering_words

We met after we had fallen in love.
Our friends wondered if that's possible.
And now as the world closes again,
From us they are learning how to keep love alive.

Durjoy Dutta

She was a new admission,
always a black screen on the Zoom call classes.
Broken webcam, she used to say in the sweetest voice.
I never saw her before I fell in love.
Had I seen her,
I would have stopped myself
and deemed her a goddess.

Durjoy Dutta

What makes our romance special is that we don't really need anything else besides each other. From deriding the 5 star hotel's gourmet to praising the *pani puri* on the roadside food stall, material things never really mattered to us. Her sparkling eyes was the gift I got when I surprised her with bed tea in the morning. That's how simple our love is, that's how special our romance is.

_hitesh_chhatani_

Our last-minute plan became our first kiss. The loud music and shots of glittering bitter liquids weren't as intoxicating as her eyes, wandering in search of an escape. We sneaked out of the party and walked on the beach. As awkwardness gave way to deep conversations, a hug turned into a soft kiss. No loud hoots or cheers. The winter breeze and the gentle sound of waves is what made it perfect.

srishtification

Our last-minute plan was to marry in a court. Our parents approved our marriage. They are planning our marriage since 3 months. But we felt that we don't want to spend money on this, instead we can use it to help others. We convinced them. All that matters to both of us is each other's love and happiness.

ushakonduru

Our last-minute plan of a picnic under the stars turned out to be one of our best dates. Both of us lay cuddling on a blanket under the star-lit sky, enjoying the feeling of being in each other's arms. As she lay counting the stars on a new moon night, I realized that my moon was right next to me.

shivie_03

He smiled mischievously on the phone screen when I told him I was hungry during the break between my duties as a doctor and hung up promising to see me at dinner. Just then a box of my favourite snack, chocolate and sanitizer came in through the hands of a staff. I couldn't help but giggle as such surprises weren't new. At different parts of the world, we were socially distant but romantically connected.

sinjini12

Our last minute plans of attending a spoken poetry contest changed our lives. I decided to surprise him by refusing and then secretly attending it, but got surprised instead. "Life is a puzzle and it completes with a piece of love. Mine stands there, hiding behind the chairs. We are pieces of two different puzzles, but you complete me like none other. Will you be mine, forever?" "Yes, always!"

harshitagupta_16

Just like a fairy tale, our story was also too good to be true for people.
House party did for us what ball room did for Cinderella. Instagram was the postman for our letters. Also, I wasn't a frog but my princess' kiss certainly made me feel like a prince. Cheesy pickups and bollywood, like romanticism made us a fable in life.

_hitesh_chhatani_

This year our romance started with an obsession of buying plants. In two months, we filled our home with different varieties of plants. Lockdown happened and while taking care of the little leaves, a flower called love bloomed inside our hearts.

harshitagupta_16

Somewhere between, a love story that started with just an eye contact and continued with hangouts. And a love story that started with lockdown and continued with virtual meets. The only thing that remained constant was the wish to last the love story till eternity.

wordz_dreamer

His happiness confided in bringing her, her favourite flower every day after work, humming her favourite song to have her sing along and lurk. Love confides in that gentleman who still after 50 years of marriage does the same, brings her, her favourite flowers and hums her favourite song even after knowing her grave won't sing along.

ancwbb

"Hey, we don't have any recent picture of us together." She sent a message with a sad emoji. Within a few seconds came a reply. A screenshot image of their last video call.

rashmi_rekha_roy

Hair done. Mascara on. Perfect lips. All dressed up. Her mother asked where was she going even though lockdown was on, she smiled and switched on her laptop. Felt closer even though they were far. Missing each other, they kissed their screens. A perfect online coffee date made their day.

garimaaa1103

We talk less but understand more in silence. Instead of chocolates, *pudin hara* does the trick. Flowers are replaced by policies and romance happens over *adrak wali chai* and *pakode* at home if kids are playing outside. After years of marriage, the language of our love certainly has changed, evolved.

elorarath

It was a cold and dark movie night with colleagues, and my first date night with her too. As she laid her head on my shoulder, I turned a little towards her, feeling her breath on my neck, I looked at her admiring her beauty. My heart thumping like it'll blow up, romance unlocked when she locked her arm around mine.

a_shade_of_black_

Gazing at stars and listening to ones favourite song makes sense of where my heart and soul belong . . . "hold on! I still want you". The song had been on constant repeat on her iPod leading her way to a flashback of memories. She was never able to read a single love story, so life gave her one of her own to remember.

tiwari_tanu

She - "What if lovers were named after seasons?" He - "Then we would be winter and spring. I will kiss you gently like a snowflake, envelope you with my magical charm and slowly, we will fall in love and blossom."

artscribed.tales

We made it up to our first date in this lockdown. He FaceTimed me, I received it eagerly at the first ring! He made my favourite Espresso for his drink and I made a cappuccino, which was his favourite too. Hours passed with our endless talks and the next thing I know is my morning getting beautiful with his calls and texts every day.

___aishu2905

Being in love for more than a decade now, we realized that love knows no boundaries. No matter where you are, if you're in love, nothing seems far. Well 2020 too did not change anything for us. Earlier he used to caress my forehead to make me sleep. Now he kisses his webcam. Not physically, but virtually we were together!

dikshagupta_97

ENGAGE

2020 taught us that romance was all about care you show to each other. No meetings, no physical contact, distance . . . but then also the small, cute efforts that you make can do wonders! It can create a bond that you will cherish for your lifetime.

sbhumika_2000

2020 taught us that romance cannot be tamed, it cannot be taught, its not just what movies and novels teach you. But it's what the two people make out of the moments they spend together and even when they don't.

spoken_by_heart

2020 taught us that romance isn't how close we are but that love, which never dies even though we're distanced from each other. Wearing his favourite hoodie, baking her favourite cake, working out together on video calls . . . phone calls going super long. Having no patience to meet each other. Listening to love songs. 2020 taught us the real meaning of love. ❤

kriti25__

From seeing each other at work every day to working together from home on video conferences, we kept our spark alive.

anunuvsharma

Sneaking letters from the backdoor got replaced by leaving poetic texts on the phone. Modes of expressing our love had to be modified while practising easiest ways of saving lives. And through it all, we kept our spark alive.

theinsomniacguy

From recommending songs to each other to listening songs that reminds me of you, we kept our spark alive.

sakshiii__25

During stormy days, he'd bring in the sunshine. And on days he felt lost, I'd show him the way. Through pixelated screens and virtual hugs, we kept the spark alive.

simmmraaannn

Those 3 am conversations and our happy faces over video calls had brought us closer to one another and I couldn't have asked for more.

protima_ghosh_

Those 3 am conversations defined what it is like to be with someone you can call home.

trinasaha64

Those 3 am conversations include us sitting in our windows, looking at the night sky and whispering into the phone.

dineshdaredevil

Those 3 am conversations were best paired with our shared playlist. Listening to your favourite songs makes me feel you are near.

aaaaaaaaashi

Those 3 am conversations turned me into a realist; thank you for showing me the real world from your eyes when I couldn't see it for myself.

diproborouwa

❤ Those 3 am conversations were like a scene out of a romantic movie. That passion, that fire, that feeling – it can't be faked.

harvajonsing

Those 3 am conversations became the language of our soul. We would tell each other all the good and bad things we had felt throughout the day.

var_un839

2020 taught us that romance wasn't in big things or places – it was a simple feeling and all you'd to do was take care of love and it'd bloom.

adarshyadav_official

2020 taught us that romance which keep your hearts together even if the distance is long . . . that romance in which distance doesn't matter, only feeling does. 🖤🖤

hidden_sunshine_20

2020 taught us that romance is ordering his favourite desserts to his address when he least expects it.

swikriti_gadre

"2020 taught us that romance comes with hope, the hope of seeing your love the next day, the hope that brings you joy and comfort, and the hope that heals you from miles apart."

mahiii6114

2020 taught us that romance isn't about physical intimacy or coffee dates. It's about those late night phone calls and skyping each other till they fall asleep. Romance is nothing but an emotional connection!

aaroo_doshi

2020 taught us that not even distance will stand a chance against two soulmates from being one. It's the universal beauty.

ibf_search23

My thumbs hurt from all the swiping.
If Tinder and Bumble were syllabi,
I had finished it.
I looked up
and there was
my neighbour
and I felt stupid, and stupidly in love.

Durjoy Dutta

She saw him in the balcony,
Sweating in a home workout.
For months, she thought he would say Hi.
It took him 6 months,
A weight loss of 32kg,
To find the courage to say Hi.
And she told him,
She liked him anyway.

Durjoy Dutta

2020 taught us that romance was a feeling – home was near and heart felt tighter whenever they texted.

manish.kar.167

2020 taught us that romance is not only limited to physical presence but it can still give you butterflies through that screen with virtual hugs and flying kisses.

tanijain2060

2020 taught us that romance can be as simple as waking up alone and sleeping to their voice on call.

kahintorashid

2020 taught us that romance is not in grand gestures, but in being with them through calls and texts amidst office meetings and deadlines.

aswathylakayil

2020 taught us that romance was in the little things that made your day much better. You cared for each other and you knew they did it all to keep you happy.

gopalsutradhor2000

2020 taught us that romance is immortal. We can always find new ideas to show the people how much we love them, we just have to care enough.

sunidhi211

2020 taught us that romance lies in the little things right from waiting for his message to sharing the biggest news, video calling just to see him snore to going on a virtual shopping date. Distance means nothing, when someone means everything.

heta_1609

I woke up to a text, "Date night?" on a five-inch screen, we made confessions of love.

ronvir_ray

I woke up to a text, "Let's go for an evening jog." Going for runs, and then slowly falling in love over conversations, lockdown couldn't have gotten any better for me.

shawon_mondol_in

Our love in 2020 did not need validations. We knew we were enough for each other against anything and everything.

nihalkhanna98

This year was you, me, and our small house that had very little access to the outside world but we made it anyway because we had each other.

cutekityever

Timezones apart but we still are connected through the strings of our soul.

meenakshi0202

Timezones apart but we still did whatever we could to feel closer. I'd zoom out of google maps and see us that we are only inches apart. ☺

sanju_singh2021

He pulled her towards himself, and whispered in her ears, "I cannot tell this to you sober so right now it is. I love you." For her it was the best surprise ever.

tulidas198

Video calls are sufficient for us to maintain the love story. They kept telling themselves. But one day, he surprised her by going to meet her with a mask on. It was the best surprise ever.

bijoy_singh_1

We are powerful. I believe in the power of love, he told her. She smiled at him. The relationship did have power. The tenth year anniversary was the testimony. His gift for her was the best surprise ever.

ankul_roy_

She asked him to stay quiet as she was trying to think what to do with each other. He pulled her close and told her that it was all gonna be okay, for them it was the best surprise ever.

sanjaya_roy2021

He used to get her dark chocolates every weekend when they would meet. She would smile and take it. And on those days, we find love all over again.

cherydinsta

He put a blindfold on her eyes, and brought her to the first date spot. She smiled because she was now gonna go through 10 years of memories all over again.

rohit.kumar135

The distance between them kept decreasing as the days to the lockdown getting over kept decreasing. Once they kissed, their memories of college came all over again.

rohi_chakraboti2021

She held his hand and kissed him as if nothing else mattered in this world. Her being in love with him irrevocably was our new normal.

monirsgallery

She kissed me on the lips before I could even say anything. Random kisses at random times was our new normal.

rohit.kumar135

The support from her was overwhelming, even if it was a phone call, she would make me smile. Supporting each other in stuff was our new normal.

sahilghosh12

I woke up to a text saying your favourite food awaits your presence. This distance did not stop him from giving me the best surprises.

tonni_roy_

Her food habits are mine now, and I know she has adopted mine. Long-distance makes you do all this to make a part of them reside within you.

rohi_chakraboti2021

'Are we going for a long drive today to our favourite spot?' she asked.'How can I say ever miss a chance to be by your side?' he answered. ❤

kashishalkareem7

It appears to be a dream.
You and I
holding each other.
I'm out of words looking at you
As your eyes gleam.
We move to the mellow beat,
Redefining love.
Feeling the heat,
As our bodies meet,
We dance,
Like the world's at our feet.

heartfelt.poetry_

He read all the unsaid, backspaced fears among the
bravely enunciated victory texts and still chuckled
on his phone while writing "I am proud of you".

ridhima_2009

We were away from each other but those video calls at night felt like he was always by my side … if darkness frightened me … he was the light of peace who was always abide with me💗💗👀

__tripsss.__

Late night video calls, me wearing his hoodie that smells like him, we were far away but it still felt like I was surrounded by his arms.✦

the_black_star_00

From sharing memes to sharing secrets, we fell in love on the Internet.

simarsingh_17

His dimple and my blushing face both were hidden inside the mask but still each time we met, we fell in love with each other's eyes. 👀❤

starhawker

"She's family" you introducing me to your dog, that still gives me butterflies.

eshna__gupta

My grandpa died yesterday. He was a love icon who talked about love like flowers and rain. But his own love died 8 years ago, my grandma. Today, I found his diary whose last page said "I am coming to you Lila (my grandma). Hope you remember our love that still gives me butterflies."

jigyasamishra_

As if, the whole universe conspired me to fall for him, I was spontaneously witnessing his breathtaking eyes when he greeted me with that magical upward inverted curve on his lips. My eyes, being disobedient, started romancing every inch of his face. For the first time, I felt like being hypnotised, and that still gives me butterflies.

theuncagedsoul

He grabbed my hand and pulled me in between his arms. He brought his head next to my ears and whispered, "Maybe not forever but can we just stay together and let the God decide our destiny?" That still gives me butterflies.

ll.janyaya.ll

Those 3 am conversations that we had on the rooftop where we shared our feelings, where every word was listened to without being said, was exactly the moment where my soul fell in love with yours.

worldbehindspeks

Those 3 am conversations are my favourite memories of our love. Conversations that were prolonged because we'd refused to cut the call, even after saying goodbye for the umpteenth time. On days that the missing hit harder, these conversations were comforting assurances of the proximity, despite the distance.

shwetha_2105

Our parents
wanted a big wedding.
We lit a candle on zoom and went around the
computer.
Unknown to them,
we have already completed a year
of being husband and wife.

Durjoy Dutta

He cooked for the new neighbour and her parents,
When they were down with sickness.
It's been a year
And he's still cooking elaborate lunches
For his wife's family.

Durjoy Dutta

From wishing for your hugs, to actually being hugged. The "in between" timespan in the past months, led to an even stronger and solid bond. The delay in meeting, made us value time, and cherish every moment, without taking each other for granted. The distance didn't break us, It made us.

stutee.k

From wishing for hugs, laying down on cozy rugs, grooving on the melodies unplugged, I had a perfect date with you in my daydreams.❤

ridhima_2009

From wishing for your hugs to spending whole day with you, our love story blossomed like a flower and I am so blessed to have you! ❤ XD

sim_sachdeva_13

Miles were just numbers that our video calls outnumbered! ∞♥

shobitsandhu_

He said hey baby and I skipped a beat!
Hearing his voice gives peace to my day!
His words bring the grins on my face! The
beauty in whispered talks is something else!
And this is how our I LOVE YOU's are shared!
The best thing I get with the late night calls
is to sleep while listeing his loving voice!

ik_tara._

I woke up to a text which said, "HAPPY
SUNRISE☀️" Little did I know that that one
text was enough to make my heart smile
and my day shine.🖤

ashna tantia

First date. He wiped cake crumbs off my lips, setting off a million butterflies in my stomach. 10th wedding anniversary. He grabs me, pulls me close, wipes off the cake crumbs, smiling. And that still gives me butterflies.

thewoundedhealer

2020 taught us that romance can be the one thing that can't be changed despite physical distance; it's more about the connection of the souls.

in_the_name_of_writing

2020 taught us that romance will stay if the threads of love that bind us are strong no matter if distance separates us.

thegratifiedpoet

2020 taught us that romance is in the moments, unconquered even by a pandemic!

realm_of_nitinitika

2020 taught us that romance isn't always the connection of skin, it can be sensed through souls too.

goranshigupta

2020 taught us that romance isn't always about hugs and holding hands, but also about making your presence felt in your absence. It's about the littlest of things that bring back memories of the other person, on the days that your heart refuses to stop yearning for their proximity.

shwetha_2105

We rediscovered love in late night video call date nights and movie nights. We maybe socially distant, but we were romantically connected.

simarsingh_17

When I see your face, I can feel your smile travelling through my veins directly to my heart and tickling my stomach, giving birth to all the butterflies and making me fall in love once again . . .

_pri_yanshii_

When I see your face, I miss you even more, do you miss me too, I ask myself every night, not able to forget our time together, I am stuck in those moments when you were mine, I am still yours, lost in your galaxy, not able to find my way back, I don't even want to.

tanishaagarwal0911

When I see your face, I fall in love with myself again because instantly, I dive into the ocean of loyalty that resides in your eyes.❤

ink_and_gouache

When I see your face, nothing else matter, its just u and me . . . Us against the world. ❤

_zephyr_14

When I see your face, I see you staring at me from the corner of your eyes, between your Zoom calls, when you're watching cricket, even when you are dressing up. And I tend to get butterflies every single time.

spoken_by_heart

Miles away from the each other . . . but having lunch together on a video call was love!

paaavaanii

From wishing for your hugs . . . To feeling like getting one every time, our promise never broke away . . . Not even some distance could change that feels.❤❤

scarletwitch6106

Just like a fairytale, every rythm of the wind and every chirp of the bird sang your name to me. ❤

rıdhıma_2009

Just like a fairytale, I just knew she was the one I wanted to dance all my dances with. ❤

ridhima_2009

What makes our romance special is the trust and faith towards each other though having a long distance! The virtual hugs and kisses shared has the deepest feeling in it, which gives goosebumps everytime though with a long distance!

ik_tara._

What makes our romance special is that I can't hold you but still I can't let you go. My affection for you gives me hope and that hope curses me every day. My hands touch you the way they haven't touched anyone. What can I say more?

vinya_jain

When I look into your eyes, everything freezes, the time stops and for all I know, it seems like forever on the watch with you. A forever that persists!

shobitsandhu_

When I look into your eyes, I see my every chaos calming down, I see a shine that they say exists only when you're with me.

_aaina_anand

When I look into your eyes, I can see the love and care for me without you expressing it! I feel the intensity our love has! I just wanna stay there forever! 🥺

ik_tara._

When I look into your eyes, I see a craving for me every minute and each second, and I feel to cut the long distance we have and come to you!

ik_tara._

When I look into your eyes, I don't feel the mobile screen between us.

sometimesjhalli

Lockdown was as beautiful as glowing flower. She woke up at early six for her yoga and he was woke up to receive her good morning text. They both cooked something different at their home. He cooked some spicy pulao and she made dalgona coffee, which was a trend during that period. Both shared a lot of memories and still remembering it.

introvert exploit

My kind of Love does not consist in gazing at each other, but in looking outward together in the same direction.

charvi_arora242

Meeting you was fate, becoming your friend was a choice, but falling in love with you was beyond my control.♣♥

harshitarao_18

He said he was going away for studies but little did my heart knew how much I felt for him and finally I opened my heart, we unlocked our different heart beats.

kanishka_.50

We were at a business networking event where the rule was that you were not allowed to buy drinks for yourself, whatever you bought, you had to put it into someone else's hand as an opener to conversation. So this gorgeous girl walked up to me, put a gin and tonic in my hand, and introduced herself. Now, we are planning our wedding.

aaaryan_jaiswal

"Do you think it's okay for you to make my heart flutter and act like you have no idea?" I asked.
"What are you saying?" she asked.
"I am trying to say don't show your beautiful smile to others, keep it reserved only for me." I said, sounding totally jealous.
"Okay, I won't!" she blushed.

words_by_khushi_

Her smile is the simplest miracle that she can create anytime.

singhaaryan07

They told me that to make her fall in love I had to make her laugh. But every time she laughs, I'm the one who falls in love.

abhishekkkk___3

Feelings and passions I couldn't pursue, Yet I kept my eyes open, Heavenly cupid finally struck its dart, I realized it was you, Who was always in my heart.

prasha.reads

It was love at first sight.
On the first day of counselling,
They had planned dates to go on, places to see.
But now they plan zoom meetings,
And realize love's
Really all what they said it to be.

Durjoy Dutta

She left the town when she joined college.
He too did that a year later.
They kept saying they were homesick,
Only to realize what it meant when the college
shut down,
And they came back home to each other.

Durjoy Dutta

Even in between weak signals and different time zones, we kept our spark alive through messages, memes and virtual movie nights.

rahulbhardwaj_2

From seeing each other at work every day to working together from home on video conferences, we kept our spark alive.

anunuvsharma

Times hit us differently. I didn't like early mornings. She didn't enjoy late nights. So, we became each other's 11:11 wish and we kept our spark alive.

puja.roy_12

Those 3 am conversations remind me of your warmth. These conversations are as precious to me as our first hug.

meenakshi0202

Those 3 am conversations and staying up a little longer was like walking an extra mile because I knew you were worth all the trouble.

ritu_sharma526

Those 3 am conversations we had were always punctuated with yawns, giggles and unsaid 'i-love-you's' and yet, there's nothing I would ever change about them.

ballisticbutcher

I never had much to say, but in those 3 am conversations, I told you all my secrets and we had much to discuss. You kept me happy and I called you mine.

malik_daniyal_rehman

2020 taught us that romance is mostly easy, and comes effortlessly when you are with the right person.

rohan_barma7

"You know what's attractive?" Efforts. When someone actually puts in efforts to see or talk to you, that's attractive.

devoted2books

Everyone in college was addicted to coffee. He wasn't. "I don't need coffee to wake up and get started for the day. Her smile is enough to recharge me. She's my everlasting cup of coffee."

thatsmall_towngirrl

"They were listing beautiful creations of nature. "Waterfalls" "Moon" "Your smile" he said. She blushed and had a soft smile on her face. "That is it. I become crazy looking at them."

tv.ramakrishna

2020 taught us that romance is hypnotic. It's fascinating in its own way. Others think we are crazy, but they don't have to get it. Our romance makes sense only to us.

.jaisss.

2020 taught us that romance exists, we realized we liked each other during a rainy day. It was drizzy for the whole day, we were sitting in a cabin on the terrace and he went down to bring me cup of ginger tea. It was windy so he offered me his jacket. It was a special day! 2020 taught us that romance can happen anytime.

kartikeya__mundra

2020 taught us that making the best of time in hand is the world in hand, as we progress in life towards each other, holding tight for a while in time.

maata_yolo

We met on Wattpad, as lovers of the same book. We took our words to mail to messages. And our heart took it from brain to mind to heart. It was love at masked sight.

shubham20_02

We were both musicians and we shared what we were best at---music. Somewhere in the middle, our random mind songs transformed into full-fledged serenades. But I knew, one day, that it was love at masked sight.

avanireads

At a mask-erade party, where the masks had to have the cheesiest Covid themed pick up lines. Mine read, "Hey Maskali, were you masked in heaven for me?" Hers read. "Better a masked devil than an angel without a mask." We were declared winners. And on that day as her laughing eyes met mine, it was indeed "Love at masked-sight".

hued_soliloquy

If I had to choose between breathing and loving you, I would use my last breath to tell you I love you . . .

jainesh131

Every day taking a walk to a workplace never felt so beautiful before we bumped into each other one day and since then our eyes bumped into each other speaking what the heart had concealed.

sanskriti077

There was a boy who was playing in the street when he saw a picture on footpath. He kept the photo but forgot about it until he was married. His wife asked who is that little girl in his wallet. He answered, my first love. Then his wife smiled and said I lost this picture when I was 9 years old.

_its_gauri

I never believed in love at first sight. Until when he held my hand and took me to other side of the road. The warmth I felt when he touched me was indescribable. I didn't stop him and kept going as if I wanted this. I felt completed and wanted to spend that moment with him. We did and till date we are spending years with each other. ❤

rushalipopli_

I wrote a poetry for him, and he unplugged himself with every word, the poetic language attached our strings, and we danced all along together on the beat of each others hearts. And that's how, this lockdown, we unlocked our love story, by being each other's voice, talking with eyes.

palakjatwani

Our love in 2020 was a blessing because my heart bubbles with excitement when anything reminds me of you. I am filled with great joy whenever the thought of you crosses my mind.

sahilaarya77

Our love in 2020 has strengthened and became even stronger, she is messy but cute, ahh, her anger and her tantrums but I take them all because she is the reason of my smile, she is the absolute reason of me being so strong to face the world with anything, this year, we got no opportunity to meet but that doesn't affect our bond in any way.

iamxofficial07

Our love in 2020 made me realize that, If I had but an hour of love, if that be all that is given to me, an hour of love upon this earth, I would give my love to you only. I love you that much.

rao_baleshwar33

Our love in 2020 made me realize that if I could ask God one thing, it would be to stop the moon. Stop the moon and make this night and your beauty last forever.

mauryakhurana07

Our love in 2020 made me realize anything happens tomorrow or for my rest of the life. I am happy now . . . Because I love you and and you love me untill the end of universe.

arora.gautam11

Our love in 2020 put together the most unexpected love with the unexpected person at an unexpected time.

talented_tharki

Our love in 2020 was more beautiful than a summer sunset on the ocean horizon. You are more breathtaking than the lush landscape on a mountain. You shine brighter than the stars in the country sky.

debukaharsh

Our love in 2020 was like a cup of coffee; the more I drink, more I fell in love.

sarthakmalhotra3

Our love in 2020 was a tough one. A constant push and pull. Somedays we weren't enough, the rest, we were too strong to be trapped inside a room. Yet day by day the person inside the head and I learnt to love one another, yet again.

_anchorage

We were strangers with different prospective, met online, fallen for each other online, we decided to meet at last but then tragically lockdown happened and again back to online chats, but it dosen't affect our bond in any way.

bhawna_bharti0682

Our love in 2020 wasn't as ordinary. Meeting was on a webinar, we dated 'virtually'. He smiled, I blushed . . . And it came to an end with, ". . . AM I AUDIBLE TO YOU?? "😂😂

__shruti__412

Our love in 2020 was filled with lots of ups and downs because we were not able to meet each other. Video calls, calls, messages were not enough. But somehow we managed to keep our relationship and love intact and celebrated the New Year together with lots of love and happiness.

_shrutii_kashyap_

Our love in 2020 had all new levels of mad we couldn't even have imagine. Seeing each other became laggy and physical affection became error 404 not found! But no one can separate two persons bonded by oxytocin so here we are in 2021 as weird as first met and as loving as every day.

yadavashish._

Our love in 2020 is like a battle between doing FaceTime and making time to meet face to face. Being in a relationship is not so easy. Prioritizing is not so easy. But loving someone is not so tough. The day I met him, my life was fully changed. Even if we have to face the challenges, we'll overcome together.

sanah_malhotra20

Our love in 2020, divided by pandemic but united by memories. We crossed the bridge of distancing and reached across the sea to the coast of 2021.

bhavna.10

Our love in 2020 was full of memories, adventure, fights, like every other relationship, it is not a dream story and in practical world complimenting disparities is what we call love. ❤

janisoberoi1

Her parents switched off the internet,
when she stopped attending zoom classes,
and said rather be a tiktok star than an
unemployable engineer.
From the boy next door,
she got her Wi-Fi,
her first fan letter,
her first socially distanced kiss.

Durjoy Dutta

Sitting at home, bored, scared
they vented out on Twitter.
He leaned right,
she leaned left.
They met in the centre.

Durjoy Dutta

Those 3 am conversations showed us a different side of each other, the vulnerability that is hidden during the day, even from those closest, and brought us closer than ever.

sana.gupta192

Those 3 am conversations, those never ending calls were like desserts, it wasn't for whole life. But the taste was unforgettable.

kk.h.u.s.h.i

Those 3 am conversations were all we had in 2020. When you are apart, love hits on another level. These were the only thing that saved us and took us one step closer.

hiiiiraeth_

Those 3 am conversations, that rush of emotion, of love, that comes over me so swiftly, it's like a wildfire in my soul. I hope you know how much you mean to me, how much I love you, and how excited I am to walk through this life with you.

debukaharsh

Those 3 am conversations help us put our guards down and bring out those hidden layers of our personality, it's literally the time when you speak your heart out. 3 am isn't just a time, it's a feeling.

prernamadaan_

Those 3 am calls were the only thing keeping us sane throughout the lockdown ... We got accustomed to sleeping during the call, listening to each other's voice and also hugging a soft toy all night wishing it was him ... Those 3 am conversations truly were a bliss. 🖤🖤🖤

say_cheese05

Those 3 am conversations makes my world glow. It makes the sunrise, the winds to blow and the rain to fall. This love is beautiful.

sahilaarya77

Those 3 am conversations, aren't they just beautiful! Those career and life planning with your other half, those sneak out phone calls and those sleeping while having conversations with cuddling. Cozy and positive vibes. Convinced that you'll always have that 3 am person with you.

vidushighosh

Those 3 am conversations were literally the best. The heavier the eyelids, the sincerer the words and silence is not awkward, it's all shared!

priyanshi_nagpal22

Those 3 am conversations slowly started getting longer. It was no longer a thing we had to do, not a ritual we used to find peace in.

piyushpandey_27

It was my first virtual date experience and yeahh I loved it though I was chatting with many random girls but there is only one in my heart and she is super special to me; she is sweet, innocent and a complete package of beauty with brain. I met her on Instagram and there I just fell for her.

ajiteshrai7

2 am video calls: Our virtual dates were and are always romantic, full of laughs and continues with teasing each other. This 2020 lockdown has made us realize that its not the physical touch but the emotional touch and connection that make a bond beautiful and true.

mitaligupta_

Two strangers swiping right and left on Tinder and then they come across each other's profile and what starts with awkward conversation and later transforms into compitition of awkward cheesy pick up lines, we are all set to have our first phone call! It's the one I'm waiting for, Damn.

being sumitt

The first ever virtual date that we had was just a delightful experience. He looks at me for a moment as if he had found something he had always cherished for and had lost a long time back.

sgar_sharma

Virtual date, first experience for me. I was ready in my best outfit but was really nervous and felt the butterflies in my gut. We both were nervous in the beginning but still ended up talking for 3 hours straight, that too virtually.

pr.ern.a

Virtual date, first for us! Meet request was sent and I had butterflies. She came and switched on the camera; at that moment I felt everything around me just paused.

varnwal_rupesh

First time talking to a stranger online, first time rooting for someone's happiness who was faceless, first virtual date, a concert.

_anchorage

They were talking about the Virtual Class Meet which ended up as a Virtual Date. 🖤🥂

jayesh_manwani

We're just friends, is what they said. But their smile said something else.☺❤

jayesh_manwani

I can't believe that you are mine. When I first saw him, couldn't take my eyes off. That naughtiness in him gathered all my attention. He didn't even realize when he became my life. The journey was amazing, from high school sweetheart to official life partners! ❤ It took a pretty time though.☺

silkyseth_

I became a complete mess this year but having him beside me made it better. I thought I needed to sort everything going on but as he came along, he helped me realize that I am a beautiful mess. ❤

gaindad

You were like a new book I was drawn towards at the library. It wasn't love at first sight. With every chapter, you grew on me and I didn't even realize when you turned into my favourite.

king_mehta100

ENGAGE

I know of no greater happiness than to be with him all the time, without interruption, without end. The more I think it over, the more I feel that there is nothing more truly artistic than to love him.

shruti_sakhuja

Virtual date, first time I got the chance to get ready in this lockdown. I was all decked up to just see one glimpse of him.

rohitchauhan007____

She met him as a stranger on Instagram but now he's the most important part of her life. No video calls, no long calls but listening to each other's favourite songs. Yes, that was there first virtual date!

parnikajain

From shyness of holding hands on our first date to tightening the grip on fifth, the spaces between our fingers were filled forever. ♥😊

arorapratima

Last slice of pizza, we smirked at each other and the story began. So, a lot can happen over a slice of pizza. 😆🍕

___srishti25

She's why I wake up in the morning. She's all I think about when I go to sleep. And it's only her hand that I want to hold—the only hand that fits my mould.

blade.exe_gaming

When we met—we couldn't stop looking at each other. Now—we never stop thinking of each other. After all these years—we've never stopped loving each other.

gauravvasija

The first time I saw her, I agreed that I was scared. But something about her smile made me realize she was the one for me.

__shazam_7

"When he looked at her, he realized he was right. She did not look like nice or pretty. She looked like art. And art isn't supposed to look nice, it's supposed to make you feel something." And everything about her made him feel something.

har.shit.ahh

Online gaming date on video call even though I am awful at them but it makes my lover laugh and that's where I find the meaning of love when we both laugh together.

pallavisingh_02

Meeting you was like listening to a song for the first time and knowing it would be my favourite.

d_e_e_p_a_l_i_

I choose you. And I'll choose you over and over and over without pause without a doubt in a heartbeat. I'll keep choosing you, don't care if it's covid, social distancing or lockdown, you are always mine.

mr.rohit_7281

It started in lockdown in the most unexpected yet a beautiful way. You know that feeling when you finally meet the one you were looking for all your life. Everything feels right when you find that person and gladly I found mine.

nimishjuneja

Two souls met 200 miles apart, on a virtual date. The first time they saw each other, their eyes glazed. Fell in love, never to be separated again.

bhavna.10

You were like a new book I was drawn towards at the library. It wasn't love at first sight. With every chapter, you grew on me and I didn't even realize when you turned into my favourite.

viidhiiiiii_

The tight hug after 5 months of lockdown made them realize the value and strength of their bond.The feeling to never leave and forever be the way they are was mutual and that's what made their relationship more special.

jahanvii.d

The world locked down,
they both doubled up on their videos,
one filmed Shein hauls,
the other touted minimalism,
after an Instagram live together,
one filmed how to wear a saree ten different ways,
the other how to get good deals.

Durjoy Dutta

They had broken up.
Long distance relationships don't work.
But with everyone stuck at home,
they realized quickly,
that if your long-distance relationship doesn't work,
nothing will.

Durjoy Dutta

In this era of swiping right and left, my heart swiped for the right one who made me look for the rainbows on the cloudy days.

kshitijq11

I once asked him about 11:11. He replied with a smile that it is more than just a timestamp where I wish a dream, a dream which is not hard to believe, a dream where I am with you and you are with me.

a.kshita__

First virtual date . . . You never know, when, where and how but yes you can fall in love with most unexpected personality at most unexpected time through unexpected medium. You may not be able to explain what you feel about him . . . About us. It's just the way he takes your heart and takes you to a place where no one else can.

swatidubey_18

She was digging soil for planting while humming a song, when a car came to halt and a boy emerged out to help her. After his work was done, he smiled at her and left. Her eyes followed the car till it was no more visible. By then she had forgotten the song she had been humming.

oyepragati

I loved her in ways I didn't know I could. Her bright eyes were enough to make me leave everything and just stare at them. Her smile was one to die for. Her giggles were the reason I cracked lame jokes for. Didn't realize anyone can be so perfect while being themselves. Virtual date, first. This is just the start.

zukerbugg

We felt love and it was as good as it could've been. Together we dreamt of all those lovely scenes. But now we love and touch hearts through the screen. Seeing each other smile, that's all we truly need. I guess that's all what true love means. ❤

mohitrohilla30

A red rose on his table, a scented candle on hers; their first virtual date was nothing short of ethereal. Romance is a seven letter word, to which the gap of seven seas is immaterial.

instadles

Put your hand in mine, Let's climb up the mountain, Eat the blue sky with two spoons, Then we'll put out grey clouds, And throw them around, As if they are water balloons, And sit under heart shaped tree.

ankitarya_04

My all favourite cafés and those late night virtual dates. You were the one. You were the first and probably be the only one to know me upto this extent. I opened myself, in and out. But maybe, it's the almost that hurt me this time. You were almost-fair to me and maybe I-trusted-you-too-much.

randomscribbler

"Same lips red, same eyes blue . . ." playing loud, and a glass of red wine, enlightening the dimly lit room.Aroma of roses, filling the thick air. A quick smile is enough to steal his words followed by blush. "Is chocolate still your aphrodisiac?" As tears run down her kajal smeared eyes, she said, "Why is heaven so near, yet so far?" Chorus goes on, "We're just two ghosts swimming in a glass half empty . . ."

inourgooddreams_

With her beginning to cook recipes of my hometown, I also slowly learned to write her letters every day, around family this lockdown we didn't need to search for our time alone.

_thoughts_unplugged

We met multiple times but never really knew each other. We frequented the same gym and you seemed like my type. I knew you were quite a bit older to me but I quite liked you. It was love at masked-sight.

theweirdindiangirl

What makes our romance special is the very fact that we understand the meanings of our unsaid lines, we know when we ain't fine even if we say we are.

thegratifiedpoet

What makes our romance special is we believe that there's nothing like loving too much!

realm_of_nitinitika

2020 taught us that romance is in the little things that lead to bigger decisions, like spending the lifetime together. ❤

realm_of_nitinitika

He was her sunshine, while she became his night breeze.

spoken_by_heart

From wishing for your hugs to snuggling against the warmth of your love, I realized that my heart had followed the right direction, to its favourite destination.

shwetha_2105

Sharing the same headphones, listening to the same beat, we drove for hours to reach nowhere. That nowhere was the most beautiful place!

shamitabehl

I remember vividly, the day we confessed. I said, "I love you", you replied "I love us", that still gives me butterflies.

uttarambhia_

Under the dark sky, within the calmest long drive, beneath the beauty of twinkling stars, we glanced upon each others favourites, you and me, got drowned more into our love. ✦❤

fatima.maryam_

She would look at me and laugh and that would make my day; she making my day, it was our new normal.

akash_sing_2

She held on to my fingers as tightly as she could. I smiled and told her I was not going anywhere. Love was our new normal.

kumar_das8

"The price is a lot to pay for your dreams,"
she looked at me and said. I smiled, "For
you, I would do it all over again."

beeyondboats

Timezones apart but we still made each
other smile and laugh after a long day at
work. He knew that sharing his stories were
the only thing that could put me to bed.

mohi.tsharma321

Timezones apart but we still know each other by heart as if our souls are intrinsically intertwined. Even the tricks of time can't stop us from gravitating towards each other. I believe love has the power to transcend all the time in this world.

swatygirish

Our love in 2020 was like a winter morning sunshine—soothing and fulfilling.

teacupteachingsllc

I woke up to a text from him and I realized why we're so good with each other, we are in love, we just didn't know it yet.

amit_gosh_in

2020 taught us that romance is supporting each other in tough times. Sometimes just a call or a text from them is enough to make your day.

cute.cat.feet

2020 taught us that romance was being able to achieve all the things that you've been keeping bottled up in your heart for that one person.

rainbowsweety3287

Those 3 am conversations. Our sleepy voice. Our heavy hearts. I knew it was love.

shritidebnath

Those 3 am conversations was more than just a time – it was a bond that we were forever knotted into and we couldn't get out of that place alive.

avajitroy20

From helping you cross the road to holding your hand forever, we kept our spark alive.

soura_bhgawade

In a world full of home deliveries, I want you to be my Swiggy order which covers the distance and brings the food to me.

rohit.kumar135

2020 taught us that romance can be even virtual too ... Can be just smiles and support even from distance ... Can be an amazing support for your good mental health ... Can be just some silence to feel the balance and ignore the violence of life. Can be just someone adorable even in the worst phase to make you realize how amazing you are!

wordztorlite

Lounge pants replaced bodycon dress, maggi took place of fancy foods, actual greetings turned into technical glitches. We watched a murder mystery together on Netflix. Never thought a virtual movie date could be this great!

b.l.u.e.m.o.r.p.h.o

From sharing memes to finally having time to talk, we reconnected. My long lost best friend and I talked like earlier college days, sharing burnt photos of tried parathas to vibing to the same old favourite songs at our homes, 2020 taught us that best friends can never stay apart even if life's changing!

khushbuthakker28

From sharing memes to finally sharing the lyrics of our most favourite songs, we realized we had come a long way. Now we also share the restaurant bills and the electricity and internet bills and the house rent. We share a home, we share love! ♥

totshotsbyanubha

From sharing memes to finally cooking for each other while locked in, from having comfortable silences to invigorating conversations about books, both of them realized that they had found their "one" amidst the chaos that had engulfed the world.

nidhijohari_

When they locked the society gates,
When she couldn't go back to her city,
He felt a guilty, uncertain joy.
Surely, she would go back once it all ends.
He would check the statistics every day.
Probably the one in the world who
wished the pandemic continues.

Durjoy Dutta

Best friends and now lovers.
Everyone squealed at their wedding.
Two years together, every moment of
every waking moment,
They realized best friends, not lovers.

Durjoy Dutta

It's all merry when I receive gifts from everyone, yet I wait for the gift you have chosen, when you smile its warmth reaches my heart, when you listen to my tales and look at me lovingly, you are the best gift that Santa has ever given.

zainxb.__

It's all merry when there is someone to hear your stupid talks, When he threats me before he blocks, When he holds my hand suddenly during morning walks, When he likes my old post while he stalks!❤

shrishti__28

It's all merry when you bake some cookies when I come home late exhausted. It's all merry when we giggle at the lamest jokes. It's all merry when your fingers just find mine while crossing the roads. It's all merry when it's just us and love is the strongest thread that ties us together!

khushbuthakker28

It's all merry when we both open our apartment doors at exact same time to pick up morning paper and I smile at you with racing heart. But it just got merrier when your love confession slipped out of my rolled paper today. ❤

mani.arora93

This year our romance flourished by walking the seven steps of togetherness. As I hold her hand to encircle the holy fire, her fingers fill the gaps present in mine, my soul felt complete. Her smile give the rhythm to my heart and the joy which I cherish for life.

samruddhi.sharma

This year our romance started with an obsession of buying plants. In two months, we filled our home with different varieties of plants. Lockdown happened and while taking care of the little leaves, a flower called love bloomed inside our hearts.

harshitagupta 16

From being a school time crush to now a lifetime partner, from sharing memes to finally being a meme in eachother's lives, from yearning to meet to actually living together, from tight smiling skin to getting wrinkles together. It was all so delightful with him by my side. Life has been so beautiful so far and yet more to go.

shivi24.mishra

This year was you, me, our dearest phone and your beautiful memories. No matter how far we were but the late night calls and sharing each other's weird pics were some things that makes your presence feel.

khushi_belani

A normal morning until I received a letter with my favourite chocolates and flowers. Which says, "let's welcome the 'new year' with 'new us'. I want to make you mine with all the rituals. Will you marry me?" I saw outside and he was standing in front of me. I quickly hugged him and said, "happy new year" "Happy new us" he whispered.

khushi_belani

Timezones apart but smiles on our faces appeared as we watched the sunset and sunrise together at the same time, over screens. Whoever said love can't win over distances was definitely wrong.

jolchhobi.creations

He is a bollywood lover, I am a book warm, his cheesy pick up lines made me laugh, his innocent smile made me happy. We both were like the north pole and south pole, constantly attracted to each other . . .

ravenspirits_

After all the efforts she made for him, he got to know that no other woman could love him the way she does; they glittered and bloomed their love all over again! :)

___.aayyushiii.___

I woke up to a text and my heart sank. You had missed your flight and couldn't make it back in time. The lockdown happened and we were stuck. Away for months. Time passed. The heart ached. Then one day, the bell rang. No flights yet, but you had driven 15 hours to reach home. Love lifted us. In this case, across state boundaries. ♥

menenners

I still remember the 1st time we met. I was a sweet mess. Sitting in his car, not sure what to do next. What I don't remember is how we went from holding hands to holding each other's hearts. And yet today, 10 years after that messy date, he holds my hand while driving the car, and that still gives me butterflies.

rahi_doshi91

We first met at a volunteering event. Besides distributing food, water and other essentials; I saw him distributing smiles to everyone there. Although everyone wore masks, the smile could be clearly seen in their eyes. And my eyes? My eyes were blushing if that's even possible. Guess it was love at masked-sight.

drishwrites

It all started at a food festival where I was clicking snaps and he was staring at me without blinking for once. I noticed him but didn't make him feel that. I smiled at a glance and he made his head down with a million dollar smile keeping his hand on his face; the biriyani festival became a rashmalai festival for us.

an_ambivert_girl

What makes our romance special is we didn't fall out of love during this lockdown but with every call, virtual date and chat, we became more sure that we are meant to be together.

keziyyaaa

What makes our romance special is battling odds together, confronting the storms and sailing together. Our love is not expressed in words, in a language different from others because we both cannot hear the music of universe. The strength lies in being disabled and we dream of making the world disabled-friendly.

weaver of thoughts

What makes our romance special is that he leaves the last slice of the pizzas and pastries for me, be it a virtual date or an actual date. A great way of making into a foodies heart and telling them that they matter.☺

harshini_kasturi

I didn't like the goofy hearty stickers on the between app, it was so perfect that I was scared of us being together. In a new place of claustrophobic discomfort and overly loving messages giving me goosebumps, I settled for the dressed down emojis, the simple huggy, lovey eyed and blushing monkey ones. It is such a pain to experience healthy love after several toxic ones.

vasuhemadri

Our last-minute plan of watching Frozen by Disney was magical . . . Grabbing the last packet of our favourite popcorn and hot chocolate from the nearby departmental store, he became my Prince Charming and I became his Damsel in Distress . . . Once in a while, right in the middle of an ordinary life, love gave us a fairy tale.

mhk_2010

Our last minute plan was to see if we got up in the morning and then decide where to go. Neither of us were sure it would work. But sitting at "our" secluded mountain, watching the sun rise as our arms kept each other warm, we both knew no plan could have been as good as the one we didn't make.

rahi_doshi91

They'd just saw each other's silhouette in real life, hardly exchanged any words. But they vibe online like they'd met in a beehive. Ever since socially distant, but romantically connected.

pritesh.arun

"Socially distant but romantically connected" . . . this is what our relationship has always been . . . being in love since school and staying together in college does this to you! You are rarely together physically but mentally, always in each other's arms . . . Not exactly the fairytale I wanted but what's a fairytale without some drama and twists!

.nish.u.

Just like a fairytale, he came all dressed up as prince charming with his best friend and I was dressed in a pink gown as bridesmaid as it was my best friend's wedding. Looking at each other, we felt a connection and some butterflies inside, it was love at first sight. ❤

prachililaker

Food check Champagne check High speed internet check It was our first Anniversary and not having him around was a big deal for me But as we celebrated it over a video call. It made me realize that virtual celebrations can be heart warning too.

iamriyarajput

Amidst our busy schedules, between the mess so called 'work from home' with tired back and with all the rough things we were going through, we were in touch. Because distance and rough timetable can never be the source of friction between true love. Love never owes to any condition!

pampering_words

I woke up to a text, "Good morning, sweet heart. Please take care of yourself, don't skip your meals and do take your medicines on time. Also, keep calm and drive slowly to work." For me, this is the only wake up alarm I rely upon and probably the only medicine which make me smile.

Soumyajeet Pal

Online dating was never my thing. I would find it absurd how people could do that. I wasn't even searching for love when I met you. I don't need to know how but it did happen. Friendship that turned into care and then into love. So slowly I couldn't even notice. Not for once. I question my decision. Your presence assures me every time.

singh_reads.kanwar2

Talking to someone who makes you laugh all day long, who doesn't want that person in life, I got the beautiful person in lockdown, pandemic never felt so good as she was there for me with me.

koko.islove

"Let's have a picture together," she said.
Both smiled.
Screenshot taken.
Beauty of Long Distance Relationships.
And together they survive the bad days of lockdown
beautifully. ❤ 🌷 ✨

yukta_pareek

This year was you, me and our fights for no reason. The
healthy ones, the love for each other, the care for each
other has made us grow through our thicks and thins.

kanchi.spammm

This year was you, me, and experiencing everything.
We both were afraid of being broken again,
but together we entrusted each other. Opened
our hearts and look where it got us. We get to
experience the most magical feeling in the world.

aanvi_writes

This year was you, me and the zoom online classes
which brought us together. Seeing you in the
online class every day in the morning made my
rest of the day fresh. I took the courage to text you
personally and that was what made the year for me.

bookish_minion

This year was you, me and our promises of loving each other till our last breaths. I am glad we got married, to have found my soulmate in you and have someone to call my own now.

harshibibliophile

From waiting outside your tuition centre to meet you to waiting for your online class to end to video call you, I came to know that love always finds ways.

rimachak2604

This year was you, me and the fact that we helped each other grow throughout the lockdown. Instead of letting this lockdown get between us, we constantly motivated each other to get the best out of us.

shruti_zunje

I believe that getting addicted to a voice is a thing. You may not hear the voice on a regular basis but whenever you do, you will surely feel butterflies. Loving a person comes in a lot of ways, mine is this. Only now I know that this can happen on a regular basis. I am glad to be able to hear this voice throughout the day because of online work.

sameeksha_reads

A mistake,
An accident,
She unknowingly broadens her Tinder search
age to 50.
A man her mother's age,
Likes her mother in her profile,
And years after her father's death, love finds her
mother again.

Durjoy Dutta

For him, the shyest guy of all time,
he had words to charm her, not the confidence.
The pandemic was custom made.
She was already in love by the time they met.

Durjoy Dutta

This year was you, me and us giving time to our hobbies. It had been years since I sang my favourite song and a decade since you last played the guitar. To learn all of that again together with you makes me such a happy person. We are back as the singing duo again. Indeed this pandemic brought us closer.

ask_vibes

This year was you, me and the terrace of our homes which let us meet every day from across the road. Chatting with you all day and secretly tipping out to the balcony and having unsaid conversations for minutes was what made this year special for me.

damon__boi

This year was you, me and our art together. I never realized that I was falling in love with you with every turn you took while dancing. Every move of yours captivating me, making me play my tabla with much enthusiasm. It's like every beat I play is meant for you to dance on.

myshittypencil

This year was you, me and our promises of loving each other till our last breaths. I am glad we got married, to have found my soulmate in you and have someone to call my own now.

cutepieeee

We got closer this year and forever. Soulmates come in the form of friends too, it's not just about romance. Sometimes, it's your best friend who makes you feel whole and who understands you the most when the world doesn't understand you at all.

confessions_of_a_bookoholic

We got closer this year and memories are always special, sometimes we laugh by remembering the days we cried, and we cry by remembering the days we laughed. That's life.

t.a.n.a.v.i

We got closer this year. I still remember how I used to wait for you by the bus stop every day. I never expected you to talk to me, but your glimpse was enough to make my day. And here we are today, together for the rest of our lives.

kvmoorthy3470

☺We got closer this year because you got me painting again. It has been years since I painted someone's face but when I looked at you, I knew your face deserved to be preserved on a paper. You got me painting again, seeing which you got attracted to me. What a year of renewing skills it was!

bongreader

They had been best friends since age five. She was head over heels for him but so were other girls. She needed to confess before someone took him away. Gathering her courage, she went to him and said, 'I think I need a new heart. It has stopped working ever since I saw you.' 'You can have mine then.' He wound her in a tight embrace and smiled

rahul.s_ig

"She didn't have a different notification tone for his messages, but even without seeing, she would know, it's him and smile."

Jay_mahakal////

2020 taught us that romance is not just staying together but being together in all the rough and smooth patches without holding any grudges.

samruddhi_sheth_desai

2020 taught us that when two souls are meant to connect: location, timing and circumstances are irrelevant. We suddenly become a magnet for one another and despite their efforts to fight it, the universe somehow manipulates it all in their favor.

pm_hansraj

2020 taught us that romance is sharing emotions. However, he came into my life and somehow wiggled inside my heart. I began opening up to him. With him it was easy to talk and open up about feelings. I never feared that he would judge me or have a low opinion of me and that's when I realized that I have fallen for him.

sight.unseenn

Our eyes met through that masked face. We would see each day during our evening walk and fell in love. It was love at masked-sight.

storiesbybharti678

We were supposed to get a new manager but the hiring was delayed. We were happy as it meant one of us would be promoted to the post. However, soon someone was hired and it made me really angry as I was one of the contenders. But when she entered the cabin wearing a mask and hipster glasses, my heartbeat increased. It was love at masked-sight.

yourstrulydebasish

The society had appointed a new secretary. My car was scratched at the parking lot right the next day. I went to him to argue over his mismanagement. However, the moment I saw him, my anger melted away. He was helping the guard with unloading some good. That muscle man in a mask stole my heart away. It was at masked sight.

inevitable.words

One evening during an office dinner, he saw her looking at the sky. 'What are you doing?' She smiled at his question and replied, 'I am checking to see if the star beside me is the brightest or do we have a competition.' He laughed at her words and hugged her hard. It was love at masked-sight.

motivationaldailythoughts

We were 10 when I picked up a fallen leaf of Gulmohar tree and gave it to her with my confession of love. She took it, giggled and hid her face with hands. We grew up, matured, moved on and married different people but fallen Gulmohar leaves lying on the roadside is one of the things that was love at masked-sight.

unexplored.territory

One thing that 2020 gave me was you. An unplanned surprise in the most unusual way. You were like a present wrapped up in a mask. It was love at masked-sight.

cutepieeee

I was never a foodie, but after being with him for over three years, even with the distance between us. I have picked up his habits. Now we both share the love for food together.

fictional_world_love

One afternoon we were talking on the phone and because of the distance it was our usual schedule. He mentioned about his favourite food that I didn't know about. Later that evening I had it in front of my doorstep. I knew I chose the right one.

gangwalmeghna

She was new to the country and felt lost until she met Aman. The boy did everything possible to make her feel at home. From laughing with her to cooking food from her nation, he did it all. And one day the distance between them was not there anymore. She became his forever.

shefali_a.1120

He would always surprise me with a mixed playlist of our favourite songs together. Listening to them now after decades, they still give me the same feeling. That still gives me butterflies!

prasha.reads

He loves braiding my hair. It is our tradition every night, he never learns to do it the right way, but he never misses a day; that still gives me butterflies!

jalsworld

She sends me random texts throughout the day saying how she misses me. Even though we spend half of the day together, her cuteness makes me weak. That still gives me the butterflies!

readwithmadhu

I always wanted to go to places unknown, adventurous, romantic and full of surprises. The day when you surprised me with the tickets to Manali, I was so happy. So happy that it still gives me butterflies.

_r_a_j_234

We would always sneak around to talk and meet each other. I remember the thrill and excitement I felt before meeting him. Now after being together for years, that still gives me butterflies!

_aswathichandran

It was our first date. We went to a downtown cafe. He sat opposite to me. I felt a little awkward looking at him, but as I raised my head to look into his eyes while conversing, I found him staring at me mesmerized. This sight made me instantly blush and gave me butterflies.

coffeewithtales

We were colleagues in the office and having a relationship between colleagues was strictly against the laws of our company. So we kept it a secret until we decided to get married. The news of our marriage shocked them all. We knew we were good actors last of all. We returned to office after marriage and the smiles and eye contacts when we were a secret still gives me butterflies!

v_kituu

"After the long tiring day when I went to bed, I found him still awake. "Not feeling sleepy," I asked. "I was waiting for you," he replied and wrapped me in his arms. "You must be tired today" he whispered and kissed me on my forehead. As his lips touched my forehead, he held me tighter, giving me butterflies.

shayanrajput123

The way her eyes spoke to me was different. It was a language not everyone could decipher yet my heart knew instantly what she wanted to say. Amidst the whole crowd of the college, you held my hands that day and made sure people knew that you belonged to me. i keep playing that moment in my head on repeat; that still gives me butterflies.

dop_shahnawaz_sarkar

She's my beacon of hope. She gives me a direction when there's no path to be found. Her care for me. That still gives me butterflies!

esha.lovestoread

"Slowly when you wrapped your arms around me this morning just before leaving, whispering sweet words and I love you in my ears. The memory still gives me butterflies.

amresh_rai8

He has a habit of always surprising me. He leaves little notes all around for me to find and read them. His loving nature makes me fall deeper in love with him. That still gives me butterflies!

__s.a.n.j.a.n.a____

I remember we were in our school for the whole night. It was the night stay! There were teachers, batchmates. We were young only. When we all got dressed up, he was the first one standing outside my door to say that I looked beautiful. Between the chaos he found me and asked me to dance. It's been 2 years now, that night still gives me butterflies.

susmita_sen243

Do you still love her? Asked his friend. I don't know but I utter her name a hundred times a day. How? I could not find any better name for my daughter from hers. He replied with a blissful smile.

Singh Robin

After a terrible fight she hung the call angrily saying, Don't call me again, I don't wanna talk with you. A few minutes later, a messaged flashed on her phone, If you don't wanna talk, we can chat right? That's when she realized how lucky she was to be with him.

Jayant Agarwal

"This year was you, me and a glorious, colourful autumn.We'd just left the coffee shop. When we walked by, she had giggled and pulled me inside, saying, "C'mon, let's be basic white girls and get some pumpkin spice!" I don't like coffee. I never had. But when she handed me my cup and looked into my eyes while I tried it, it was the best thing I'd ever tasted.

Kethi Garg

He was a Twitter handle.
No picture, no bio,
But his tweets kept her awake.
His retweets of her pleas to get her parents
admitted kept her hopeful,
And when they first met,
He promised to keep her feel loved.

Durjoy Dutta

This is not how she had imagined love at first sight.
He peers down his nostrils,
His eyes watering,
His face obscured by his mask,
And yet,
That's how it happened.

Durjoy Dutta

This year was you, me, and the experiments with food that we did together. Each day we downloaded the recipe and tried to cook a new dish. It was all experiment; hit and trial that made me look forward to the dawn of the next day as soon as the first one ended so as to cook something amazing new.

Meena Jain

"This year was you, me and Starbucks. I was waiting for my coffee at Starbucks and a really handsome guy came next to me to order. I whispered daamn it was louder than I thought. He looked at me and said" "I was thinking the same thing".

Kulbhushan Rajguru

This year was you, me and the second half of the season, winters. Our favourite food tastes best in winters. Our coffee breaks get a little longer, the cuddles don't stop, won't stop. To share a plate of Maggie feels divine. Got saucy soup of tomatoes, they taste so fine. Every winter I enjoy being with you, living with you, in the same house.

Nayna Bansal

"This year was you, me and last night. Last night I thought he was sleeping so I whispered I love you just to see what it felt like. Nothing will ever make me feel as good as it did when I heard him whisper," "I love you too baby".

Ishika Malhotra

He said as he finished his book reading, "Love works in ways us mere mortals can't comprehend or describe. It can only be felt together with someone." She was sitting in the first row smiling and looking at him. She knew he wrote it for her.

Swati Shah

"We got closer this year and as you were new in the town, and I was the one who gave you a detour of the city, I have been living in this city since my childhood but, this city never felt this beautiful to me, I think it was the company of yours that made this happen, I love exploring the new corners of this city and you."

Shivraj Uthale

"Let's video call?" She said. "No, mom is sitting next to me."
He replied. "Ughh, we both will mute the call, just look at
each other's ugly faces and talk to each other through eyes.
I just want to see you, missing you a lot." She said. "Haha, I
love you for this one, give me a call."

Syed Usama

"What a day it was, we should take a picture together", asked
the girl to his boyfriend, "Why just a picture let's create an
album of us", Asked the boy with a ring in his hand.

Kanwarpal Singh

After playing in the rain for the whole evening they came back, and he gave her his t-shirt, "Are you comfortable in this?" he asked. "it's the best", "I think you have much better clothes than this", "but none of them have this warmth."

Swatishree Jena

As I told her what I feel for, she said, "it's not possible because you are from Beverly Hills, and I am from nothing hills, everybody knows you and my neighbour doesn't even know my name", so I told her, "the only thing I want to know is about you, nothing else matters to me." She was with tears and a big smile.

Huda Shadab Shamsi

After a long chat in the night, at 2 am he asked,"are you feeling sleepy", "no, not at all", said the girl with a coffee mug and swollen eyes.

Spellboundark

I may smile at dumb pick up lines but I swear the first thing that hit me is to run away. I met a him on a bus stop, I was listening to the music and he started asking me for directions. I said use Google map, he said he wanted directions to my heart. My brain got freeze I smiled and said I was getting late.

Paromita Das

"Can I follow you, where you are going right now?" I asked. "Why? I am going to the library, and you hate quiet places," he said. "You see, my parents have always taught me to follow my heart, and right now it's with you." I said with a cheesy smile.

Khushi Tayal

2020 taught us that romance is about understanding each other and connecting with each other emotionally and whatever we do we just want our partner to be happy, and when you find the perfect person to love it's just by learning to see an imperfect person perfectly.

AAyush Rathore

They shared a cab in the first days of the virus.
They wore masks and yet came down with the virus.
She blamed him.
Little did she know, he blamed her.
Months later, they bumped into each other,
Without masks,
And the anger melted away.

Durjoy Dutta

2020 taught us that romance can do wonders, make us believe in some power that is beyond. You became so special to me just in a few days. I can see so many things without any haze. Being with him makes me weak in my knees, I feel butterflies around my head. I let my walls down with you without any efforts.

Amina Thajudeen

"Want to the beach to see the best sunrise ever," he said,"no it won't be the best" she replied,"it would be the best I promise", "no, trust me ", "then you say what would be the best sunrise", "The day I will wake up next to you", she smiled.

Kevin Shah

The sky was turning pink as I was returning from work and then I saw her, she was with her friends. I was mesmerised with her magical glow just then she looked at me and I sort off stumbled. After 30 years of our marriage and her Alzheimer's, every day I get the same aloof look and that still gives me butterflies!

D Singh

She left him at the station on 19th March and after two days, the complete nation got locked up. He was waiting for her to be back to give a meaning to the bond they had started together. They counted months and then difficulties too, but the 10 pm calls at night looking at the moon and the brightest start gave them hope of meeting again. Now, he was her moon and she was his brightest star.

ashwathi_ambili

//Captured in a library//
Engrossed in reading a love story, she forgot to notice me staring at her. While her eyes were glued to that one page, I was hoping for just one pleasing look. Years later, I was holding her hand, and she was holding our first co-authored book. I wonder if it was a mere coincidence or God's plan to get us hooked!

dhruv_dc_

This global pandemic and distance may have become obstacles between our meet up plans but it was incapable to hamper our relationship. Despite the obstacles, which was not giving us chances to meet physically, we found that our happy place lies in each other's heart!

the_scrittore